For Izzy, with thanks

HODDER CHILDREN'S BOOKS

First published in Great Britain in 2016 by Hodder and Stoughton

1 3 5 7 9 10 8 6 4 2

Text and illustrations copyright © David Melling 2016

A CIP catalogue record for this book is available
from the British Library.

ISBN: 978 1 444 93109 9

Printed in China

Hodder Children's Books
An imprint of Hachette Children's Group
Part of Hodder and Stoughton
Carmelite House
50 Victoria Embankment
London EC4Y 0DZ

An Hachette UK Company
www.hachette.co.uk

www.hachettechildrens.co.uk

D is for Duck!

(and)

David Melling

Hodder
Children's
Books

Bunny

Chicken

Duck

Fox

Goat

Hatch

Insects

Jungle

King Lion

Panic

Quick

(Quack)

Run!

Up

Vanish!

Where is
everyone?

X (Kiss)

Yuck

DUCK!